WEEKLY READER CHILDREN'S BOOK CLUB

PRESENTS

GUS WAS A FRIENDLY GHOST

by JANE THAYER

ILLUSTRATED BY Seymour Fleishman

WILLIAM MORROW & CO. NEW YORK

There was once a friendly ghost,
by the name of Gus.
He lived in an old house in the country
with apple trees and lilacs in the yard.

Mr. and Mrs. Scott
and their twins, Susie and Sammy,
lived there too, in the summer.
The old house had an attic,
and sometimes the Scotts
heard rattles and clanks in it.
That was Gus.
The Scotts didn't believe in ghosts,
so they didn't believe in Gus.
Still, when they heard
the rattles and clanks
they liked to say to their friends,
"We've got a ghost!"
The Scotts made Gus
feel welcome in the old house,
so Gus liked them.
He especially liked Mrs. Scott,
she was so pretty.

He wanted to please them all,
so he rattled and clanked in the attic,
the way ghosts are supposed to do.
"We've got a ghost!"
said the Scotts proudly,
though they didn't believe in ghosts.

Then autumn came and the Scott family left.
No need to rattle and clank now.
Gus had nothing to do but sit around.

One day he was so lonely,
sitting around by himself,
that he went for a walk.
And he met a mouse.
"How are you?" said Gus.
"F-freezing!" said Mouse,
with chattering teeth.
"Come and spend the winter at my house!"
cried Gus.
"Any people there?" said Mouse.
"I do hate people!"
"Not now," said Gus.

Mouse scurried about the house.
It seemed a good place to spend the winter,
but it was chilly.
"Let's build a fire in the fireplace,"
said Mouse, with chattering teeth.
"I'll get a match."
He scurried to the kitchen.
But the Scotts had taken
all the matches away,
on account of mice.

"Bother!" cried Mouse.

Gus had never built a fire.

Ghosts never get cold.

But he wanted Mouse

to be happy in his house,

so he said some ghostly words he knew,

and a fire began to blaze in the fireplace.

"Well!" said Mouse with delight.

"Let's have a bite.

I'll look in the cupboard."

He scurried to the kitchen.
But the Scotts had taken
all the food away,
on account of mice.
"Bother!" cried Mouse.

Gus had never cooked a meal.

Ghosts never get hungry.

But he wanted Mouse to be happy.

"Toasted cheese sandwich?" said Gus.

"There isn't any . . ." began Mouse.

Then he saw

that Gus was slicing a big piece of cheese.

Mouse was delighted.

Gus was pleased

that he had thought of the cheese.

Gus pulled a table up to the hearth.

He piled nine pillows in a chair for Mouse.

Mouse enjoyed his toasted cheese.

Finally Mouse wiped his whiskers.
"Which is my room?" he said.
"Take your pick," said Gus.
"Bed will feel good!" said Mouse.
He scurried into the front bedroom.
But Mrs. Scott had put
newspapers all over the bed,
on account of mice.
Mouse made a face.
"I do hate a newspaper!" he said.

He scurried into the back bedroom.
"I'll curl up in a drawer."
But Mrs. Scott had put
mothballs in the drawer,
on account of mice, of course.
Mouse made a terrible face.
"I do hate a mothball!" he said.

Gus wanted Mouse to be happy in his house.
"Try the attic," he said.
Mouse ducked into a hole in the wall
that Gus showed him,
and found his way to the attic.
He burrowed into an old mattress
and went to sleep in the stuffing.

Gus washed the dishes.
He was delighted
to have Mouse in the house for company.
When Mouse woke up
he scurried downstairs and said,
"How do I get out of here?"
"Don't go!" cried Gus.
"Aren't you hungry?"
"What are we having for dinner?" said Mouse.

Gus began to be very busy.
Mouse liked his three meals a day,
with nibbles in between.
So Gus put on an apron.
He got out a cookbook.
He looked up all the things
a mouse might like to eat.
He spilled sugar all over the floor.
He got flour all over his face.

He burned his fingers.
But he made macaroni and cheese
and cheesecake.
He whipped up cheese soup and cheese sauces.
He baked cheese bread and cheese biscuits,
cheese popovers and cheese pie.

Mouse never had time to help,
he was so busy with various matters.
But Gus didn't mind.
Mouse grew plump on cheese sauce.
At night when it snowed,
Mouse read to Gus by the fire.
Sometimes they played checkers.
Sometimes they popped corn.
Firelight flickered on the old windowpanes
and smoke curled up the chimney.
No one was near to notice.

But at last the snow melted
and the sun grew warm.
The buds on the apple trees swelled.
The lilacs burst into bloom.
And one day a car drove into the yard.
The Scotts were back.
When Mouse heard Susie and Sammy
running through all the rooms,
he ducked into the hole in the wall
and rushed to the attic.

When he peeked out of the mattress
and saw his friend Gus,
he cried angrily, "I'll scare them away!"
"Why? They're nice!" said Gus in surprise.
He was glad to see the Scotts,
especially Mrs. Scott.
But Mouse had been so happy in the house,
with Gus's cooking and everything,
that he was furious to think
the Scotts had come and spoiled it.

Gus couldn't cook
with Mrs. Scott in the kitchen!
So Mouse scampered down to the parlor
when the Scotts were playing checkers.
He ran back and forth inside the wall,
patter, patter, patter, patter, patter,
to scare them away.
"We've got a mouse," said Mr. Scott.
But the Scotts weren't scared away.

"What do you want to do that for?"
said Gus to Mouse.

Mouse paid no attention.

He scampered into the kitchen.

He nibbled a piece of blackberry pie
and tracked the juice around.

He chewed open
a box of marshmallow cookies.

He spilled some tapioca.

"Behave yourself," said Gus.
Mouse scampered into the bedroom
and chewed a hole in a pillow for good measure.
But the Scotts weren't scared away.
So Mouse scurried up to the attic
after the Scotts were in bed,
and stamped about over their heads,
making all the noise
a mouse could possibly make.

Finally Mr. Scott said,
"I'll set a mousetrap."
The next day
Mouse saw a new thing in the attic,
and smelled something good.
He was so hungry!
His nose quivered.
He crept closer . . . and closer. . . .

"Keep away!" cried Gus.
"It's cheese!" cried Mouse.
"It's a trap to catch you!" said Gus.

He put up a sign that said *Danger*.
When Mr. Scott didn't catch Mouse,
he set another trap,
then another.
Gus kept putting up signs that said *Beware*.
"Why can't you folks get along?" cried Gus.

But the more mousetraps Mr. Scott set,
the more Mouse stamped about
among the danger signs,
to scare the Scotts away.
Gus began to be really worried.
He didn't want
his friends the Scotts bothered
and he didn't want his friend Mouse hurt.
"I'd never forgive myself
if *anything happened,*" he said.

Then one day Mouse became so determined
to scare the Scotts out of the house
that he popped up on a kitchen shelf,
bold as brass,
when Mrs. Scott reached for the cereal.
"Help!" screamed Mrs. Scott, running away.

That was the last straw.
When Gus saw Mrs. Scott,
who was so pretty,
scared out of her wits,
all of a sudden
he pointed his finger at Mouse
and roared, *"That's enough!"*

Mouse was so shocked
that he stood stock-still and stared.
"Listen to me!" shouted Gus.
"If you stay in this house,
you'll do as I say from now on!"
"What?" whispered Mouse.
"You'll stop scaring Mrs. Scott," roared Gus.
"O.K.," said Mouse meekly.
"You'll stop nibbling and chewing.
You can go out in the garden
and eat nasturtium seeds," shouted Gus.
"O.K.," said Mouse.
"You'll keep quiet
while the folks play checkers."

"I'll walk on tiptoe," said Mouse.

"You'll stop stamping around the attic.

I'm the only one

allowed to make a noise in the attic!"

"I'll be as quiet as a mouse," said Mouse.

"All right!" said Gus,

with a sigh of relief.

Then he saw how meek and scared Mouse looked.

"It's just till the folks go away,"

he said kindly.

So Mouse tiptoed about the house,

and ate nasturtium seeds in the garden.

The Scotts said, "That mouse is gone."
And Mr. Scott took away the traps.
Gus rattled and clanked
extra loud in the attic,
so the Scotts could say,
"That's our ghost!"
And when the Scotts
went away for the winter,
Gus and Mouse had a celebration,
with cheese croquettes for dinner!